Pebble®

Families

Mothers

by Lola M. Schaefer

Consulting Editor: Gail Saunders-Smith, PhD

CAPSTONE
press®

Mankato, Minnesota

Pebble Books are published by Capstone Press,
151 Good Counsel Drive, P.O. Box 669, Mankato, Minnesota 56002.
www.capstonepress.com

1 2 3 4 5 6 13 12 11 10 09 08

Library of Congress Cataloging-in-Publication Data
Schaefer, Lola M., 1950–
   Mothers/by Lola M. Schaefer. — Rev. and updated ed.
   p. cm. — (Pebble books. Families)
   Summary: "Simple text and photographs present mothers and how they interact
with their families" — Provided by publisher.
   Includes bibliographical references and index.
   ISBN-13: 978-1-4296-1227-2 (hardcover)
   ISBN-10: 1-4296-1227-4 (hardcover)
   ISBN-13: 978-1-4296-1756-7 (softcover)
   ISBN-10: 1-4296-1756-X (softcover)
   1. Mothers — Juvenile literature. 2. Mother and child — Juvenile literature.
I. Title. II. Series.
HQ759.S2735 2008
306.874'3 — dc22   2007027098

Note to Parents and Teachers

The Families set supports national social studies standards related
to identifying family members and their roles in the family. This
book describes and illustrates mothers. The images support early
readers in understanding the text. The repetition of words and
phrases helps early readers learn new words. This book also
introduces early readers to subject-specific vocabulary words, which
are defined in the glossary section. Early readers may need some
assistance to read some words and to use the Table of Contents,
Glossary, Read More, Internet Sites, and Index sections of the book.

Table of Contents

Mothers

A mother is a female parent.
Mothers have children.

daughters

mother

son

6

At Home

Nina's mom makes breakfast before she goes to work.

Ty's mom reads to him
at bedtime.

Eddie's mom mows the lawn.

12

Work and Play

Alice's mom teaches
piano lessons.

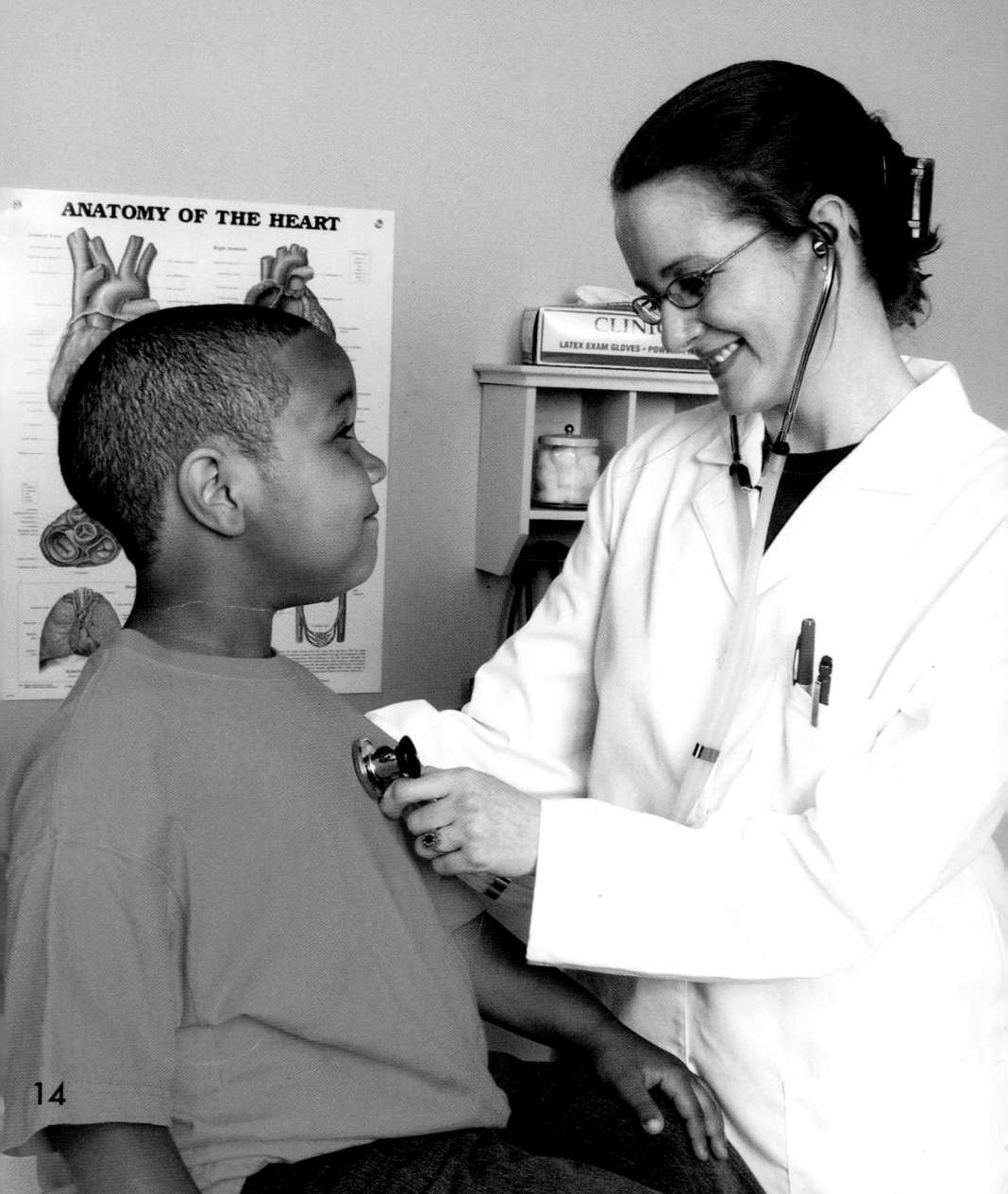

14

Al's mom is a doctor.

16

Andy's mom watches football.

18

Grace's mom golfs.

Mothers love.

Glossary

lesson — a set time for teaching a certain skill

mow — to cut grass; mothers do many chores inside and outside.

parent — a mother or a father of one child or many children; when a parent has more than one child, the children are called siblings.

teach — to show someone how to do something new

Read More

Easterling, Lisa. *Families.* Our Global Community. Chicago: Heinemann, 2007.

Sirett, Dawn. *Mommy Loves Me.* New York: DK, 2006.

Internet Sites

FactHound offers a safe, fun way to find Internet sites related to this book. All of the sites on FactHound have been researched by our staff.

Here's how:

1. Visit *www.facthound.com*
2. Choose your grade level.
3. Type in this book ID **1429612274** for age-appropriate sites. You may also browse subjects by clicking on letters, or by clicking on pictures and words.
4. Click on the **Fetch It** button.

FactHound will fetch the best sites for you!

Index

Word Count: 49
Grade 1
Early-Intervention Level: 10

Editorial Credits
Sarah L. Schuette, revised edition editor; Kim Brown, revised edition designer

Photo Credits
Capstone Press/Karon Dubke, all